For Sophie Bea, who loves reading books xx
— L.R.

For Lillington Library - where my love of picture books began
— B.M.

First published 2022 by Macmillan Children's Books
an imprint of Pan Macmillan
The Smithson, 6 Briset Street, London, EC1M 5NR
EU representative: Macmillan Publishers Ireland Limited,
1st Floor, The Liffey Trust Centre,
117-126 Sheriff Street Upper, Dublin 1, D01 YC43
Associated companies throughout the world
www.panmacmillan.com

ISBN 978-1-5290-0367-3 (HB)
ISBN 978-1-5290-0368-0 (PB)

7 9 8 6

A CIP catalogue record for this book is available from the British Library.

Printed in China

Written by
Lucy Rowland

Illustrated by
Ben Mantle

A Hero Called Wolf

MACMILLAN CHILDREN'S BOOKS

There once was a Wolf who
was mean and quite hard.

Who'd turned things around
with . . . a library card.

He'd made some new friends
and he'd learnt how to share,

and he now took a satchel
of books everywhere.

But . . . one day the wolf,
looking sullen and glum,
slumped into the library
and sucked at his thumb.

"There, there!" Mrs Jones said. She asked him, "What's wrong?"
As Wolf began howling, "I just don't belong!

In all of these stories I'm always the crook!
Can't a wolf be the hero? The star of the book?"

Mrs Jones pondered, then nodded her head.
"So write one!" the clever librarian said.
"A pen and some paper – that's all that you'll need.
You could *write* the story that you want to read."

Could *I* be a hero? Wolf thought to himself.
He looked round the library and searched through a shelf.

These heroes are HANDSOME.

They're TOUGH and they're STRONG!

I can't be a hero.
I might get it wrong.

With that came a knock and a swing of the door.
The woodcutter! (Wolf knew this hero for sure.)
"I've got a big problem," the woodcutter said.
He flexed his STRONG muscles high over his head.

"My axe isn't working.
It won't cut my wood.
I might need a new one.
Oh, this isn't good!"

But then, Wolf remembered
a rather good book,
called 'All About Axes'.
He said, "Take a look."

The woodcutter thanked him and started to read,
while outside a knight had arrived on her steed.
This hero was shiny. She looked rather TOUGH.
She rushed through the door in a bit of a huff.

LET THERE
BE KNIGHT!

I ♥ U

"Well, someone has stolen my feed bag, of course, and now I can't use it to feed my poor horse!"

But Wolf could remember a farm book he'd read, and said to the knight, "Use my satchel instead."

The knight thanked the wolf.
She'd just started to read,
when in rushed a prince
(and he ran at such speed!).

A fast, HANDSOME hero with long, flowing hair.
He sulked to the others, "This doesn't seem fair!
I've got a grand ball tonight. Oh, look at that!
Someone has ruined my best feather hat."

Just then Wolf remembered a craft book he'd read.
They made a long feather from paper instead.

"Oh, thank you!" the prince cried. "My hero!" he said.
Then Wolf grinned a grin and he scratched at his head.
"A hero?" Wolf whispered, (he turned rather pink),
"Yes, maybe . . ." he said, as he started to think.

But suddenly . . .

BOOM!

Such a thunderous sound.
The shelves shook and tremored.
Books fell to the ground.

There came a loud,
"Fee!" a loud, "Fi!"
"Fo!" and "Fum!"

"Outside!" Mrs Jones yelled,
"The GIANT has come!"

"Stand back!" cried the woodcutter,
axe in the air.

"Away!" shrieked the prince,
with a flick of his hair.

And, "Charge!" yelled the knight.
"Now, you leave us no choice!"

But . . . "STOP!"
called the wolf in a deafening voice.

For heroes are BRAVE and they're CLEVER and KIND.
Wolf took a deep breath (so he'd not change his mind).
Then he turned to the giant, his voice a small yelp,
and said, "Hello! Welcome! And how may I help?"

The giant was shocked and he gave Wolf a look,
then told him, "The thing is . . . I need a new book.
I've read all my books and I'm ever so old,
I've heard all the tales that have ever been told."

"Not this tale!" the wolf grinned.
He picked up a pen,
as Mrs Jones gave him
some paper again.

"Sit down," the wolf said, "on the soft forest floor.
I'll tell you a story you've not heard before."

"See, heroes are CLEVER. They're KIND and they're BRAVE.
A hero's defined by the way they behave."
Then, suddenly Wolf knew he'd got it all wrong.
"They're not always HANDSOME or TOUGH or so STRONG."

The woodcutter, prince and the shiny knight, too,
sat down with the giant, while Wolf thought it through.
He wrote 'Hero Wolf' at the top of his sheet
and there, on his face, spread a smile so sweet.

A hero at last! It was rather exciting!
He took a deep breath and then . . .
Wolf began writing.